Great Start!

Purchased with Smart Start Funds

WORD BIRD'S
CIRCUS SURPRISE

by Jane Belk Moncure
illustrated by Linda Sommers Hohag

THE
CHILD'S
WORLD

MANKATO, MN 56001

Library of Congress Cataloging in Publication Data

Moncure, Jane Belk.
  Word Bird's Circus Surprise.

  (Her Word Birds for early birds)
  SUMMARY: Uses a very simple vocabulary to describe
Word Bird's trip to the circus.
  [1. Circus stories. 2. Birds—Fiction] I. Hohag,
Linda. II. Title. III. Series.
PZ7.M739Wo   [E]   80-29528
ISBN 0-89565-162-9 -1991 Edition

WORD BIRD'S
CIRCUS SURPRISE

One day, Mama Bird
gave Word Bird a box
of polka dots . . .

a jar of paste,

some paper,

and a pair
of scissors.

"Make something pretty," she said.

So Word Bird made a
polka dot tie for
Papa Bird . . .

a polka dot hat for Mama Bird,

and a polka dot clown suit for himself.

"Let's go to the circus!"
Word Bird said.
And they did.

"Hi, circus."

"Balloons.
Balloons."

"Popcorn.
Candy."

"Hi, lions."

"Jump, lion! Jump."

"Hi, ponies."

"Prance, ponies. Prance."

"Hi, elephants."

"Dance, elephants. Dance."

"Hi, bear."

"Ride, bear. Ride."

"Hi, acrobats."

"Swing, acrobats.
Swing high."

"Oh. Oh."

"Balloons. Balloons."

"Here come the clowns."

"Clowns, clowns,
funny clowns."

"Where is Word Bird?"

"Surprise."

"Laugh, clowns. Laugh."

"Bye-bye, circus."

Can you read these Word Bird words?

polka dots

paste
paper
scissors

tie

hat

clown suit
circus

balloon

popcorn

lion

jump

ponies
prance

elephant
dance

bear
ride

acrobats
swing

clown

laugh

bye-bye

DEMCO